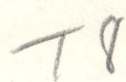

WINDOWS

THE OUTLOOKS
AND INSIGHTS SERIES
Pipes and Wires

in preparation:
Paper-making
Printing

© Rosemary and Charlotte Ellis 1975
Photographs © Rosemary Ellis 1975
ISBN 0 370 01587 8 Printed in Great Britain for
The Bodley Head Ltd, 9 Bow Street, London WC2E 7AL
by BAS Printers Limited, Wallop, Hampshire
First published 1975

OUTLOOKS AND INSIGHTS SERIES

Windows

Rosemary and Charlotte Ellis

THE BODLEY HEAD
LONDON SYDNEY
TORONTO

ACKNOWLEDGEMENTS

The authors wish to thank Michael Barclay, Henry Boys, Peter Brown, Clifford and Penelope Ellis, Mrs. I. McEwan, Katie, Tom and Simon Paterson (the builder of the arch on page 35) and their parents, Robert and Michael Pope and their parents, Charles Prosser, and the many other people who have given personal help.

The photograph of housing by the M4 motorway at Heston, near London, is by Simon Farrell, **16**, and that of offices on the Albert Embankment, London, is by Barbara Lüthy, **38**. Permission to reproduce paintings has been given by the Trustees of the National Gallery, London, for (i) *Lady standing at the Virginals*, 20 × 18 inches, by Jan Vermeer of Delft, 1632–75, **9**, and (ii) full-scale detail from an early fifteenth century Flemish painting *Virgin and Child before a firescreen*, **23**, and by the Trustees of the National Gallery of Scotland for *The Open Window*, *c.* 1899, 21½ × 17 inches, by Édouard Vuillard © by SPADEM, Paris 1974, **22**. Messrs The Boots Co Ltd provided the photograph of their 'Wets' factory at Nottingham, **15** *above*, and Messrs IBM United Kingdom Limited the photograph of their new temporary building at Cosham, Hants, **15** *below*. Messrs Pilkington Brothers Limited were very helpful at their Glass Museum, St Helens, Lancs, and provided the photograph of the louvred window in Jamaica, **12**.

INFORMATION about some of the subjects photographed by the authors:

The County Shopping Arcade, 1896–1900, (architect, F. Matcham, who also designed over a hundred theatres and music-halls), Leeds, **8**; Corsham Court, 1582, Wilts, **13**; house at Groningen, Netherlands, **14**; hovercraft: Portsmouth–Isle of Wight, **17**; Farleigh Castle, *c.* 1370, Somerset, **18**; *HMS Victory*, HM Dockyard, Portsmouth, **20**, **45**; Tryn-du Lighthouse, 1838, Anglesey, Wales, **21**; steam-railway exhibits, Haworth Station, Keighley and Worth Valley Light Railway, Yorkshire, **24**, **25**, **44**; Harewood Bird Garden, Yorkshire, **27**; keep, *c.* 1170, Middleham Castle, Yorkshire, **30**, **31**; warehouses, mid-nineteenth century, Leeds, **36**; farmhouse, fifteenth century, reconstructed at the Open Air Museum, Singleton, Sussex, **37**; IBM temporary building, Cosham, Hants, **39**; Palm House, 1844–48, designed by Richard Turner, engineer, and Decimus Burton, architect, Royal Botanical Gardens, Kew, London, **40**; *Solardome* by Rosedale Engineering Works, photographed at Helmsley Garden Centre, Yorkshire, **41**; *SS Great Britain*, 1843, designed by I. K. Brunel, engineer, who also designed railways, including the Great Western. The ship is now in Great Western Dock, Bristol, **42**.

The **Glossary**, pages 46, 47, 48, gives meanings of words printed LIKE THIS when they are first used.

Contents

Why do we have windows? 6 and 7

Letting in day-light, 8 and 9
Letting in air, 10–12
Controlling cold and heat, 13
Heat from the sun, 14 and 15
Keeping out noise, 16
Problems of speed, 17
Keeping out missiles and other things, 18 and 19

How do we use windows? 20

Letting out cannon-balls, 20 and 21
Letting out light, 21
Looking out, 22–25
Not looking out, 26
Looking in, 27
Not looking in, 28 and 29

How do we make openings for windows? 30

Lintel, 31
Arch, 32 and 33
Bridging openings in brick walls, 34
Making an arch, 35
Windows in loadbearing walls, 36
Windows in frame buildings, 37–41
Making openings in sheets of metal, 42 and 43

Windows and the look of a building, 44 and 45

Glossary and Index, 46–48

Why do we have windows?

How many reasons can you think of for making an opening in a wall to form a window?

You will know that most window openings are protected from rain, wind and snow by glass, which is kept in place by some sort of framing: this is what we usually mean by the word 'window'.

A window with glass in it is called a GLAZED WINDOW. You may have noticed several things about glazed windows: for example, glass is TRANSLUCENT (which means that it lets light through), it is IMPERVIOUS (which means that it keeps out the wet), and it is usually TRANSPARENT (which means that you can see through it). Some glass is made so that you cannot see through it easily, but it is still translucent and impervious.

Here is a view of Leeds. How many kinds of glazed windows can you see?

Letting in day-light

This is such an important reason for having windows that they are sometimes called LIGHTS. Look in the Glossary (pages 46–48) for different kinds of lights, such as ROOF-LIGHT and SKY-LIGHT.

You will be able to think of many types of building that need windows to let in light, such as schools, houses and hospitals. Have you ever been in a shopping arcade or a railway station where the whole roof was glass, like the one on the left?

The Dutch painter Vermeer has shown a great deal of light coming through the window in this picture.

Letting in air

You may know some buildings which do not have any windows. This farm silo has to be air-tight to help the grass inside change into winter food for cows. Do you know any others?

VENTILATION is needed in most buildings. The simplest way to let in air is to leave a gap in the wall.

On the opposite page there is a farm building with various ways of letting in fresh air. Ordinary bricks have been arranged to leave ventilation gaps. This is called HONEYCOMB brickwork.

A special brick made with holes to let air through the wall of a building is called an AIR BRICK. These are often used in houses and flats, and generally there is at least one air brick to each room. Are there any where you live?

AIR CONDITIONING is a more complicated way of letting in air. Air from outside comes into the building through a DUCT and is cleaned and conditioned to a comfortable temperature and HUMIDITY before being released into rooms used by people. Special conditions may be needed for some machinery, or for storing valuable manuscripts and other objects. Stale air, which has become too hot, or cold or 'stuffy', is taken out through another duct. Some of it is then re-conditioned with air from outside and the rest is pumped out of the building. If air conditioning is to be effective, air from outside should enter the building only through the CONDITIONING PLANT, so any windows will be FIXED LIGHTS.

Air conditioning is most needed where controlled conditions are essential, as in hospital operating theatres, or where the outside air is very unpleasant, because it is very cold, or hot, or very dirty. It is often installed in buildings like cinemas and supermarkets, which are used by a lot of people at once. However, electricity is used up both to condition the air and to pump it round the duct system: as electricity becomes more costly, so air conditioning will become increasingly expensive.

MORE ABOUT LETTING IN AIR

A window that cannot be opened is called a FIXED LIGHT, but a ventilator or a mechanical fan may be built into the glass. Can you see a new round ventilator in the old window opposite? Other windows, or parts of them, may open. A window may be hinged to open as a CASEMENT, or it may be pulled up and down on SASH CORDS, or it may PIVOT open, or SLIDE sideways, or a panel of glass LOUVRES may be provided. The louvres can be adjusted to control the flow of air.

Here is a window in Jamaica, a tropical island where the air is cooled by the sea. The whole window is fitted with glass louvres which can be opened to let in cool air.

Controlling cold and heat

If it is cold out-of-doors, warmth from indoors will escape unless a building is well INSULATED. If it is hot out-of-doors the air indoors can be kept cool if there is good insulation. A thick stone wall is a good insulator, because it TRANSMITS heat very slowly from one side to the other. A glass window is a bad insulator because it transmits heat very quickly.

Here are some draughty old LEADED windows, fitted with new inner windows to make a kind of DOUBLE GLAZING. There would be better insulation if both outer and inner windows fitted tightly, with a dry air space between them.

Heat from the sun

If you sit in sunlight which has come through glass you can get very hot, even when it is cold out-of-doors. Once the sun's heat has come through a glass pane, it cannot be reflected back again, so the heat accumulates indoors, and you get hotter and hotter. This process is called the 'GREENHOUSE EFFECT' and it can be very uncomfortable. It can also be useful: as its name suggests, it is used in greenhouses for growing plants.

The 'greenhouse effect' can be prevented by shielding glass from the sun, perhaps with shutters like those on the Dutch house opposite, or with blinds like the ones on the factory above. Both these methods are effective because direct sunlight is prevented from reaching the glass. On dull days, shutters and blinds can be put away or pushed back to let as much daylight through the windows as possible.

In very hot sunny weather, even greenhouses would get too hot if they were not protected. Sometimes they are painted on the outside with whitewash which reflects sunlight before it reaches the glass.

The windows below are made from REFLECTIVE GLASS, which looks like a coloured mirror from the outside. On page 39 you can see that it looks quite ordinary from the inside. Glass of this kind reflects sunlight from the outside surface, so heat does not accumulate indoors.

Keeping out noise

Noise which comes from outside a building is usually carried through the air, and will come through any opening, even a key-hole. The building in this photograph is close to a noisy motorway, and it has been designed to form a barrier which stops most of the noise from reaching the side furthest from the motorway, where the windows of the living-rooms and the bedrooms overlook a park. There are various other ways of designing new buildings to keep out noise, but it is more difficult to protect old buildings. As an experiment, some special windows were fitted to a school near an airport. These windows closed automatically every time an aeroplane approached, and then opened again when the plane had passed. This was not a very good solution because a plane passed every two minutes: the windows opened and closed each time, which was as disturbing as the noise from the planes.

Problems of speed

The name of the front window of a car tells you one thing it keeps out, and you will know all about windscreen wipers. People in car accidents could be very badly hurt if the glass windscreen broke into loose sharp pieces in the same way as ordinary glass. The design of special safety glass for windscreens has been improved: LAMINATED glass is made of sheets of glass with plastic between them, so that when it breaks, the pieces hang together. A new form of this glass will break so that the pieces have blunt edges. Windscreens are often designed with a patch which stays clear so that the driver can see out well enough to pull up safely if the glass is broken in a moving car.

When a car stops suddenly, the people inside are thrown forward, but properly worn seat belts prevent them from either hitting their heads against the windscreen, or worse, being thrown through the glass.

The windows of this hovercraft have to keep out sea-spray, and the windows or port-holes in any ship must be water-tight and strong enough to withstand the force of wind and waves.

Aircraft windows have to be very strong and well-fitting to seal the aircraft against enormous changes in air-pressure and temperature, while any windows in spacecraft must resist even greater extremes.

Keeping out missiles and other things

Castles often had windows like this one. Inside, there was enough room for a defender to shoot arrows out. Outside it was only a narrow slit, to make it difficult for attackers to shoot arrows or other missiles into the castle.

When builders first put the windows into a new building there may be a label on each pane, or they may put a dab of paint on the glass, to remind themselves that the glass is there. They have become so used to having an opening through which to pass planks, ladders and so on that otherwise they might break the new glass by mistake.

Do you know windows that need protection from anything else?

How do we use windows?

20

Letting out cannon balls

On the opposite page you can see Nelson's ship HMS *Victory*, which is at Portsmouth. It has special windows for letting out cannon balls. The cannon have covers on the ends to protect the barrels from getting wet.

On page 45 there is another part of the same ship with windows that are quite different because they had a different use.

Letting out light

Here is a building with a special window for letting out light. The light, which comes from a very powerful lamp, flashes at controlled intervals to make a signal, which can be identified as coming from a particular lighthouse. The signal from this one can be seen up to fifteen miles (about 24 kilometres) away. It helps ships at night to know where they are, so they can avoid running aground.

Looking out

Most people like to look out at a view of some sort. In this painting by Vuillard, a French lady is looking out of her casement window. There is a very different view from the window on the opposite page, which comes from a late fifteenth-century Flemish painting.

Have you ever thought of making a series of paintings from one particular window where you live? You will have noticed that the view changes with the time of day, with the weather, and with the time of year. Perhaps the most interesting change will be in the light, or the sky, or the leaves of trees and plants. If there is enough light outside for you to see some sort of view, you could do a painting on a dark winter evening. You will be able to see out more clearly if you turn out the lights indoors and wait for your eyes to adjust to the darkness. You could arrange a torch to shine on your painting.

MORE ABOUT LOOKING OUT

Drivers of trains, cars, buses, coaches, hover-craft and so on must be able to see out. The captain of a ship will need to see signals from lighthouses. Though it is possible to guide most modern ships and planes by radar, the pilot of an aeroplane may need to see landing lights and warning lights, like those on tall buildings.

Passengers on some vehicles need to see where to get out, and all passengers may like to look out at passing scenery.

You may have been in a car or bus when, particularly in damp weather, moisture forms on the inside of the windows so that it is difficult to see out.

If you breathe on cold glass, small drops of moisture will be formed. This is because warm air can carry more moisture than cold air and so, when the damp warm air is suddenly cooled by the glass, moisture is released by CONDENSATION. There are various ways of heating the glass inside windscreens to prevent this from happening.

Not looking out

In this old school the windows were put high up so that children could not look out of them instead of working.

Are the windows different in the classrooms of your school? Can you see in and out of them easily? What do you think is the best way to design windows in a school building?

Looking in

You will know many windows which are needed for looking in, for example, shop windows. Some kitchen ovens have a heat-resistant clear panel so that you can see how the food is getting on inside without opening the door and lowering the oven temperature.

We visit a place like a zoo to do a lot of looking in. You can see penguins swimming underwater through this strong window.

Not looking in

Some windows are needed to let in light without people being able to see through them.

Such a window can be made of a material that is translucent but not transparent, such as 'frosted' or OBSCURED glass, or various kinds of plastic.

What kinds of room can you think of which need this kind of window?

Here, for a start, are some obvious examples: bathrooms, changing rooms and showers at swimming baths and sports centres, bathing huts at the seaside, and examination rooms in doctors' surgeries and clinics.

It is possible to make a window from coloured glass which you cannot see through easily, but which is very beautiful to look at.

You may know a church with a window made up of pieces of stained glass which are arranged as pictures or patterns. Some houses have a FAN-LIGHT, made from coloured glass, over the front door. Can you think of any other windows made from coloured glass?

A black and white photograph could not give you any idea of the effect of daylight coming through a stained glass window. You must see it for yourself.

People who wish to see out, while not being seen themselves, may hang up curtains made of net or lace. Then, if it is lighter outside than it is indoors, passers-by will see the curtain itself without seeing through it, while people indoors can see out.

Have you noticed what happens in the evening if lights are turned on indoors? The day-time effect is reversed and it is difficult to see out from indoors, but easy to see in from outside.

VENETIAN BLINDS are sometimes used to stop people from seeing through windows. These blinds do that job well, although they are designed to control sunlight.

Sunlight coming through a window will not only make a room hot (see 'greenhouse effect', pages 14 and 15) but may spoil some of the things in it, especially colours that fade. Direct sunlight can be kept out by Venetian blinds, but their slats can be adjusted to let in some daylight.

What were the windows like in the museum you visited last? Perhaps the walls were needed for the exhibits, which were lit from above by roof-lights. They may have been hidden by translucent screens that gave a DIFFUSED light.

Perhaps some of the objects were too delicate to be lit from any window, but instead, subdued and exactly regulated electric light was used.

How do we make openings for windows?

Lintel

In a wall built of stone blocks or bricks, some kind of bridge must be made over the opening for a window. A builder's brick is quite heavy to lift—your father probably weighs about the same as 24 to 28 bricks—so a strong bridge is needed.

Opposite, a very big strong stone has been used as a bridge. The window opening on this page is wider. The large slab of stone that makes a bridge over it is called a LINTEL.

Arch

If you lean two rulers together at a fairly steep angle they will stand up. However if you then press on the top, the bottom edges will slip away from each other, and both rulers will fall flat.

The window opening on the left is bridged with a pointed arch which is made by leaning two large curved pieces of stone together. The heavy stone walls on each side of the arch prevent it from collapsing.

The parts of a wall which SUPPORT an arch in this way are called ABUTMENTS.

The impressive rounded arch on the right is made up from a great many stones, some of which have been carved into wedge shapes. They are pressed together by the heavy abutments on each side to make a strong bridge to carry the heavy masonry over the opening.

You can feel for yourself how important abutments are if you take a row of books and hold it up horizontally, just by pressing the book at each end.

Bridging openings in brick walls

The two window openings in the brick house on the left are bridged in different ways.

The bridge over the upstairs window is called a FLAT ARCH because, although it is neither curved nor pointed, the wedge-shaped bricks are pressed together by the abutments in the same way as the semi-circular arch over the downstairs window.

Window openings in brick walls may be bridged, not with arches, but with lintels of stone or concrete. There is an example of a concrete lintel in a brick wall on page 11.

Lintels made of rectangular bricks are usually supported with steel or TIMBER. Often the supporting materials are not visible from outside. The bricks may have holes through them so they can be threaded together, like beads, on steel bars. The support may be hidden by special shaped bricks.

Tiles are stuck on some concrete lintels so that they look just like brickwork.

Making an arch

First a supporting arch was made by bending a piece of card so that it was held firmly in place at each side by the bricks we used for abutments. The supporting arch for a brick or stone building is made of timber and is called CENTERING.

Next the white building bricks were placed on the centering, beginning at the sides, where we made sure that the block at each end rested very firmly against the abutments. As you see, the lower edges of each block touched one another. The upper edges were held apart evenly by rolls of paper. These were needed because our building blocks were rectangular, not wedge-shaped like those used in the building on the left.

The centering was removed very gently and the arch stood on its own. Although it is not as strong as an arch made of wedge-shaped blocks, you can see how it was tested. Four more big blocks were added before it failed. The two middle blocks slipped downwards, and the arch collapsed.

35

Windows in loadbearing walls

So far we have been thinking about openings in walls made of stone or brick. These walls are usually made so they are strong enough to hold up the floors and the roof as well as their own weight. This is called LOADBEARING construction. How many different ways of bridging openings in loadbearing brickwork can you see in the photograph of warehouses on this page?

Windows in frame buildings

A frame building is held up by a structural frame. The weather is kept out by CLADDING, which is supported by the frame. On this page you can see the timber frame of an old farmhouse, which was being reconstructed at an open-air museum. The cladding, which includes any windows, would fit between the frame timbers. The white areas added to the left of the photograph represent cladding.

37

MORE ABOUT WINDOWS IN FRAME BUILDINGS

In frame buildings that are more modern than the one on page 37, the frame is usually made of metal or REINFORCED CONCRETE. The outside walls and windows may be hung on the outside of the frame, something like rigid curtains. This is called CURTAIN WALLING. All forms of outside walling on frame buildings will be less heavy than loadbearing walls (see page 36). Sometimes, as in the office on the right, all the outside walls may be made of glass.

Each of the office buildings in the photograph below is a frame building. The frame, like some climbing frames, is made from uprights and horizontals. In these buildings, the uprights are stiffened by the floors. Panels containing the windows and walls are fixed to the outside of the frame. As the frame does all the carrying, there is no problem of bridging window openings. Different panels have been used for each of these offices, but you can still see that the floors are likely to be behind the lower part of the horizontal bands of walling. Do you think that the designer of each building has made the best of this opportunity, or would you like to redesign the panels, or rearrange them, to make a more interesting pattern?

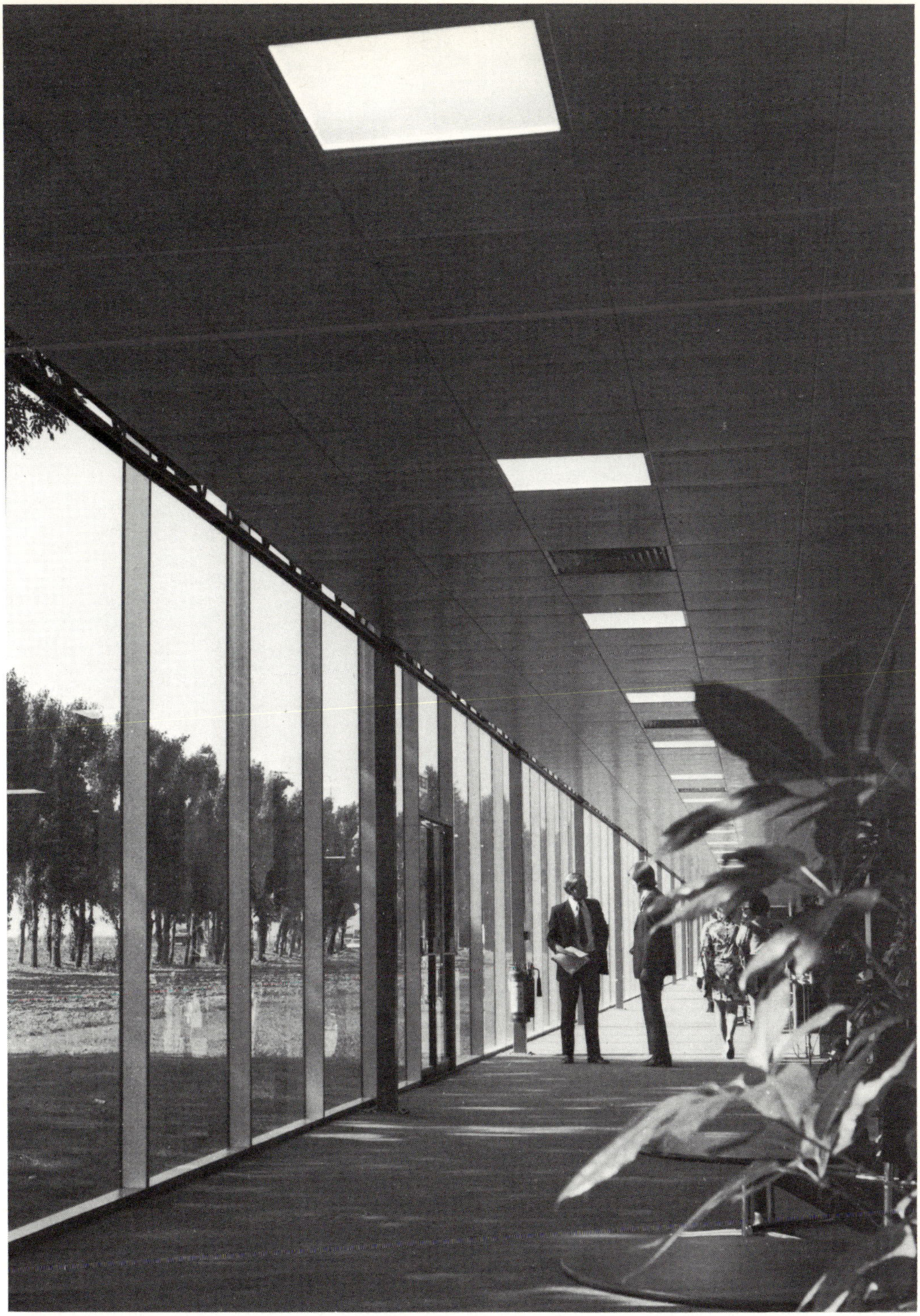

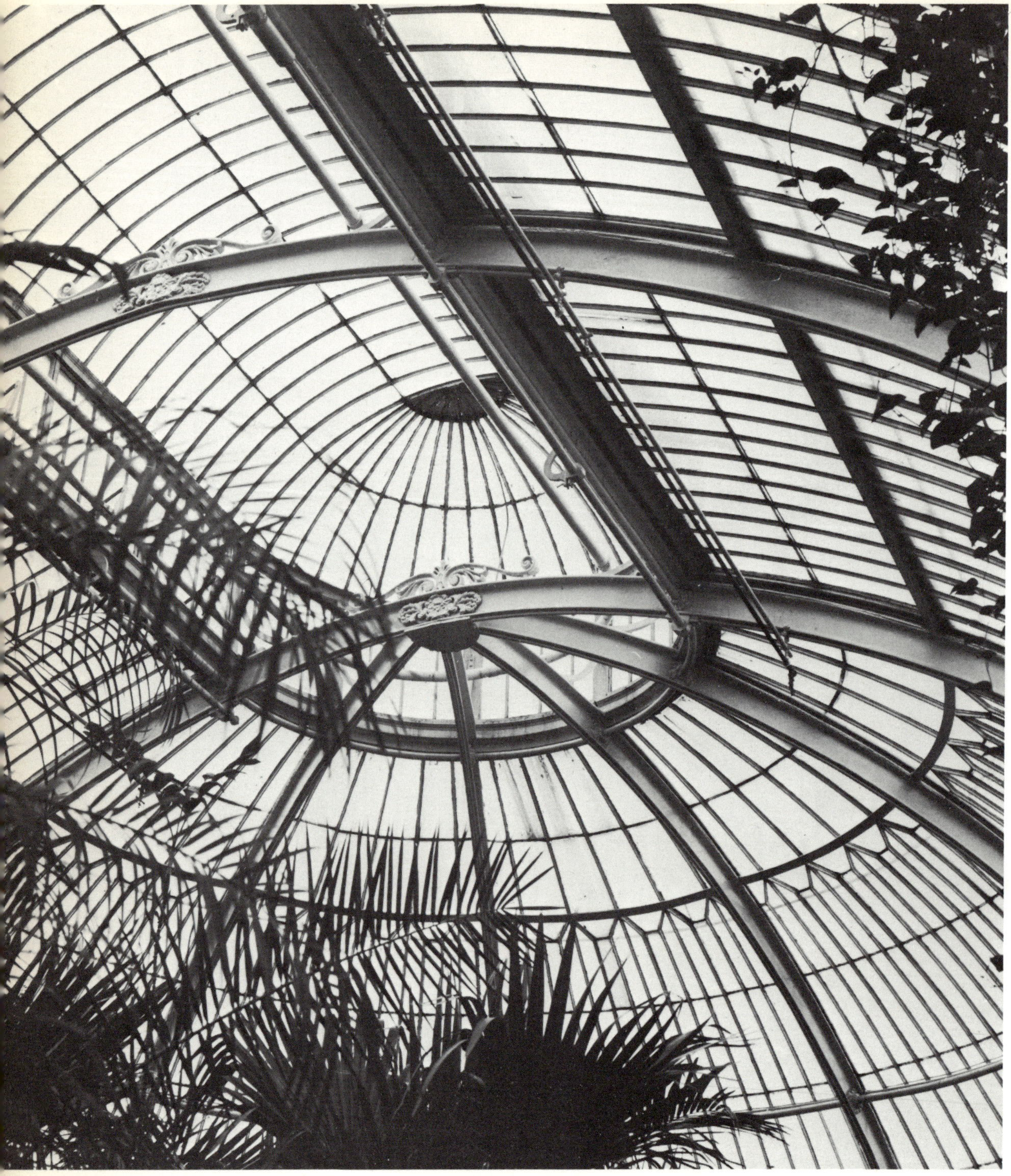

MORE ABOUT WINDOWS IN FRAME BUILDINGS

Very large areas of GLAZING can be provided in frame buildings because the frame and SUB-FRAME do all the holding up that is needed. You will remember that heat accumulates when the sun shines through glass (see pages 14 and 15), and that this heat can be helpful for growing plants. Here are two frame buildings where the 'greenhouse effect' is used in this way. All the sheltering part is made of glass so that whenever the sun shines, its heat is collected.

The big Palm House in Kew Gardens (on the left) was one of the first to have an iron frame. The strong main frame supports the WROUGHT-IRON sub-frame, which holds the glass panes in place.

The frame of the small greenhouse below is made up from metal triangles which hold the glass. You will notice that a special frame has been made for the doorway.

Making openings in sheets of metal

This is a port-hole in the first giant iron ship, *The Great Britain*, which was designed by Isambard Kingdom Brunel and launched in 1843. You can see right across the empty hull to a similar opening on the other side. The holes round the edge of these openings were drilled so the glazed windows could be bolted on. A circle is a strong shape for an opening in sheet metal, and is often used in the metal sides of things that move (see page 24).

You can make a sheet of paper less floppy by folding it into pleats. In the same way a flat sheet of metal can be made more rigid if it is pressed into a stronger shape.

You can see how the sheet of metal used to make the rear door of this van has been shaped: the edge of the window opening has been pressed into a sort of pleat. To make it even more rigid, the door is lined with a similarly shaped metal sheet turned the other way round. The soft joint which holds the glass in place is shaped like an H. It fits over the jointed metal on one side, and fits over the edge of the glass on the other side.

Windows and the look of a building

If you put bigger or smaller windows in the building where you live, or if you put in windows of the same size but of a different kind, the look of the building would be changed.

The train below has an oval window which gives sufficient protection from driving rain and from people seeing in, but you can tell, just by the look of the window, that the train was built some time ago.

Can you imagine this part of HMS *Victory* with round port-holes instead of the windows shown opposite? You can see that these windows are made of timber and not metal, but that is not all. They have the look of windows in a house—the kind of house which was thought suitable for the officers who used this end of the ship when it was built.

We have started to look at windows carefully and to ask questions about them. The more we look, the more questions we need to ask. You may have begun to notice that there are still more things to find out. You could start by thinking about the windows you know well. Are there several reasons for having each one? Does each window do all the things it should? Can you think of any improvements, or even a completely different sort of window that might be better?

Glossary and Index

The meanings given here are for words when they are used to describe windows or buildings. If you look in a dictionary, you will find that some of the words mean different things when they are used in another way, for example, the word GLAZED has other meanings when it is used to talk about pottery or cooking.

The first column on the right tells you the pages where you can find words printed LIKE THIS in the book. If there is a photograph which illustrates the word, you will find where to look for it in the second column.

	Text	*Illustrations*
ABUTMENTS Solid parts of a wall at the sides of an arch which prevent it from collapsing	32, 34, 35	32–35
AIR-BRICK A brick made with ventilation holes through it	10	19
AIR CONDITIONING A system which keeps the air in a building clean and which controls its temperature and humidity. Machinery called CONDITIONING PLANT processes the air.	10–11	
CASEMENT WINDOW A window which opens either inwards or outwards by means of hinges along one of its sides	12, 22	9, 13, 22, 28
CENTERING A temporary support, usually made of timber, on which an arch is built	35	
CLADDING An old word meaning wearing clothes, used to describe the outside covering of a frame building	37	15, 37–39
CONDENSATION The process of water vapour changing into water when damp air is cooled	25	
CURTAIN WALLS Rigid panels containing windows and walling, which are hung outside a frame building to form cladding	38	38
DIFFUSED LIGHT Light which is evenly distributed, usually after shining through some sort of screen	29	
DOUBLE GLAZING Two layers of glass with an air space between them	13	13
DRIP-STONE A moulding over a window or doorway, designed to throw rainwater away from the opening		32
DUCT In air-conditioning, a tube, which is usually made of metal, along which air travels	10	
FAN-LIGHT A window over a door. The name comes from the fan-shaped window that fitted inside the arch over a doorway	28	14
FIXED LIGHT A window which is not designed to open	11–12	
FLAT ARCH A flat bridge over a window opening, made of wedge-shaped bricks which are supported by abutments in the same way as an arch	34	14, 34, 36

	Text	Illustrations
GLAZED LIGHT A window with glass in it	7, 42	
GLAZING Another word for windows, *or* it can mean putting glass into a window frame	41	
'GREENHOUSE EFFECT' Heat which accumulates inside a building when sunlight shines through glass	14–15, 29, 41	
HONEYCOMB BRICKWORK Brickwork with ventilation gaps left between the bricks	10	11
HUMIDITY (of air) The dampness or water content of air. Very damp air has a high humidity, while dry air has a low humidity	10	
IMPERVIOUS (to water) Not letting through water	7	
INSULATION Prevention of heat, cold or sound being transferred from one place to another	13	
LAMINATED GLASS Safety glass made from layers of glass with plastic between them. When this kind of glass breaks, the pieces are held together by the plastic	17	
LEADED LIGHTS Windows made up from small panes of glass which are held together with lead. The panes are often diamond-shaped	13	13
LIGHT Any window which lets in light	8	
LINTEL A horizontal bridge over an opening in a wall	31, 34	11, 30–31
LOADBEARING CONSTRUCTION Walls made of masonry, brickwork or concrete, which support the floors and roof as well as their own weight	36	
LOUVRES Overlapping slats, made of timber, metal, plastic or glass, which admit air but keep out the rain. Glazed louvres are usually adjustable so the flow of air can be controlled	12	12, 19
OBSCURED GLASS Glass which is 'frosted' or patterned in some way, to prevent people from seeing through it	28	28
OPENING LIGHT A window which is designed to open	12	
PIVOT WINDOW A window which opens by turning on pivots	12	24 (lower)
REFLECTIVE GLASS Glass which is designed to reflect sunlight from its outside surface. It prevents heat accumulating indoors from the 'greenhouse effect'	15	15 (lower), 39
REINFORCED CONCRETE Concrete which has strengthening steel embedded in it	38	
ROOF-LIGHT A window in the roof	8, 29	
SASH WINDOW A window which opens by sliding up and down vertically on SASH CORDS attached to weights which are equal to the weight of the window	12	29, 34, 45
SKY-LIGHT A window in the roof or ceiling	8	
SLIDING WINDOW A window which slides open horizontally, along a track. Very large sliding windows may move on rollers or wheels	12	

	Text	Illustrations
SUB-FRAMING In a frame building, the cladding panels may consist of windows and walling which are held in place by sub-framing	41	15 (top), 38, 40
SUPPORT Strengthening, from the sides, above or underneath, which prevents something from collapsing	32	
TIMBER Another word for wood	34, 37, 44	37
TRANSLUCENT Letting through light	7, 28–29	
TRANSMISSION Transfer of heat or sound, through the thickness of a material, from one side to the other	13	
TRANSPARENT Easy to see through	7, 28	
VENETIAN BLIND A window blind made from slats which can be adjusted to control the amount of sunlight or daylight that comes through the window	29	
VENTILATION Circulation of fresh air	10	
VENTILATING LIGHT A small opening window over a large window		28
WROUGHT IRON Iron which is made into objects by working it, usually at a high temperature	41	40